Robert Quackenbush

Stage Door to Terror

A Miss Mallard Mystery

•

Prentice-Hall, Inc.

Englewood Cliffs, New Jersey

Printed in the United States of America

Prentice-Hall International, Inc., London
Prentice-Hall of Australia, Pty. Ltd., Sydney
Prentice-Hall Canada, Inc., Toronto
Prentice-Hall Hispanoamericana, S.A., Mexico
Prentice-Hall of India Private Ltd., New Delhi
Prentice-Hall of Japan, Inc., Tokyo
Prentice-Hall of Southeast Asia Pte. Ltd., Singapore
Whitehall Books Limited, Wellington, New Zealand
Editora Prentice-Hall do Brasil LTDA., Rio de Janeiro

10 9 8 7 6 5 4 3 2 1

Library of Congress Cataloging in Publication Data

Quackenbush, Robert M.
    Stagedoor to terror.

    Summary: In Paris to visit an old friend, Miss
Mallard becomes involved in one of the most terrifying
cases of her career centering around the disappearance
of her friend's granddaughter and the long-ago theft
of a fabulous jewel.
    1. Children's stories, American. [1. Mystery and
detective stories. 2. Ducks—Fiction] I. Title.
PZ7.Q16Sr 1985   [Fic]   84-22295
ISBN 0-13-840364-3

For Piet

On a weekend tour of Paris, Miss Mallard—the world-famous ducktective—was joined by her nephew, Inspector Willard Widgeon of the Swiss Police. They especially wanted to see Claudine Pilet, who was going to sing and dance at a nightclub called the Canard-Rouge. Claudine was the granddaughter of an old family friend, Lily Pilet.

"Isn't this exciting, Willard?" asked Miss Mallard as they sat down at a table near the stage.

"Just ducky!" said Inspector Widgeon.

A waiter took their orders and returned with two pots of tea.

Inspector Widgeon raised his cup and said, "Here's to Claudine."

"And may her success be as bright as her grandmother's," said Miss Mallard. "Lily was the toast of Paris in her day. She was courted by royalty. It was even rumored that a maharaja had showered her with gifts of jewels. True or not, she was greatly loved by everyone and sadly missed when she retired from the stage. But just imagine! After all these years, Claudine is stepping into Lily's costumes and recreating her songs and dances at the Canard-Rouge."

Just then the can-can girls ended their dancing and Claudine stepped on stage in a shimmering costume.

"Isn't Claudine pretty, Willard?" whispered Miss Mallard. "She looks just like Lily did when she was young. And the program says that she is going to perform Lily's spectacular 'Rain of Light Dance.'"

No sooner had she spoken than someone came swinging out onto the stage on a rope. He was wearing a mask. He grabbed Claudine and scooped her off the stage.

The audience was horrified. Everyone quacked loudly.

"Good heavens, Aunty!" cried Inspector Widgeon. "Claudine has been ducknapped!"

At once, the manager, Monsieur Carrot, rushed out on the stage to quiet the audience.

"Keep on playing! Keep on dancing!" he shouted to the orchestra and the can-can girls.

"Let's go, Willard!" said Miss Mallard.

"Where is our waiter so I can pay him?" asked Inspector Widgeon.

"Never mind," said Miss Mallard. "Just leave the money on the table."

They made a hasty exit. Outside, they went down a narrow alley until they came to the stage door. Opening it, they looked around. They didn't see a stage doorman, so they continued on their way backstage.

Backstage was a sea of confusion. Everyone was racing around looking for Claudine. They looked behind curtains, behind scenery, in the cellar, and in the rafters.

Twenty minutes later someone cried, "Here, in the attic! Claudine has been found!"

Miss Mallard and Inspector Widgeon ran up a winding spiral staircase to the attic. They got there just as Claudine was being untied from a post by one of the stage hands. The masked ducknapper was nowhere in sight.

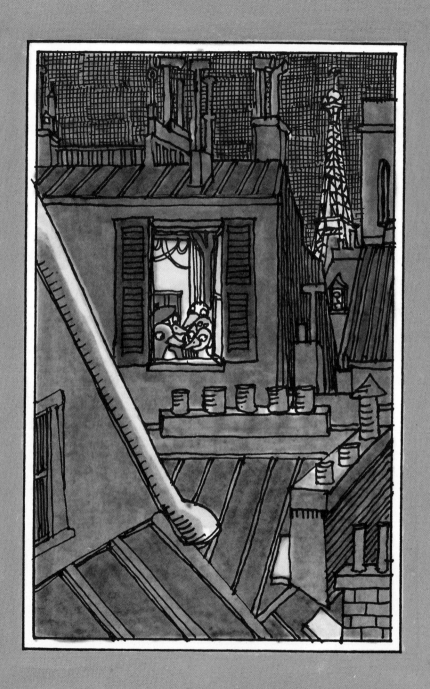

Monsieur Carrot burst into the dusty attic behind Miss Mallard and Inspector Widgeon. He asked Claudine if she was all right.

"I *will be* as soon as I pull myself together," said Claudine. "I want to go on with the show. But give me half an hour before I do. I can't imagine who wanted to mess up my act. He just brought me up here, tied me up, and left by the open window. There sure are some strange ducks in this world!"

"I'm glad you weren't harmed," said Monsieur Carrot. "I'll tell the audience that your act will be delayed. Take your time."

Miss Mallard and Inspector Widgeon followed Claudine to her dressing room. When Claudine opened the door, she let out a gasp. Everything was in a mess!

"Who did this?" cried Claudine.

She went over to her dressing table and picked up a single red carnation.

"Who left this here?" she asked.

"I think I know," said Inspector Widgeon. "The carnation is the trademark of a notorious international jewel thief. He has left red carnations all over Italy, Switzerland, and Germany. So now he is in Paris! If we could only find out who he is and catch him!"

"Whoever he is," said Miss Mallard, "he was not working alone. He had a partner ducknap Claudine. Then, while everyone was looking for her, he robbed the dressing room."

"But I have no jewels!" said Claudine. "And nothing is missing!"

She thought for a moment.

"I know!" she said. "Grandmother sent me a copy of the 'Rain of Light' costume this morning. She had sent me the real one earlier but then she began to worry that something might happen to it. She asked me to store it in a safe place until she could pick it up. Marie, my maid, packed it in a suitcase and checked it at a railroad station. Then she sewed the claim ticket in the hem of my skirt. Do you suppose that is what the thief was looking for?"

"The jewels of a maharaja!" said Miss Mallard, surprised. "So the story about Lily receiving royal gifts was true! And Lily had them sewn onto her costume to keep them safe. No one would imagine that her costume had real jewels on it."

"No one but the red carnation thief," corrected Inspector Widgeon. "He can sniff out real jewels anywhere. And with two thieves on the job, it would be even easier."

"Quick, Claudine!" said Miss Mallard. "We must get the suitcase before the thieves do. I'm sure they will put two and two together and realize that it has been checked."

Claudine made a little tear in the hem of her costume. She removed the claim ticket she had hidden there and handed it to Miss Mallard.

Miss Mallard looked at the ticket. It was torn at one corner. All that could be read was the word "*gare*." Below that was the number 44.

"*Gare* means station," said Miss Mallard. "But the rest of the name has been lost. Which station could it be? There are so many of them in Paris—not counting all the underground Metro stations."

"*Ooo-la-la*," said Claudine. "Only Marie knows that. And I gave her the evening off. We've got to find her! Grandmother would be so upset if anything happened to her costume—and her jewels."

"Where could Marie be?" asked Miss Mallard.

"Well," said Claudine, "I know that she has a friend, Helene Eider, who dusts and sweeps at the Notre Dame Cathedral. Maybe she went there."

"Let's go check it out, Willard," said Miss Mallard.

"I'll ask Gerard Tadorne, our doorman, to call you a taxi," said Claudine.

Willard wanted to see the rest of the show.

"Shouldn't we stay for a while longer and question the can-can girls, Aunty?" he asked.

"Whatever for, Willard?" asked Miss Mallard, annoyed.

They went to Gerard Tadorne's tiny glass office by the stage door. He called on his telephone for a taxi.

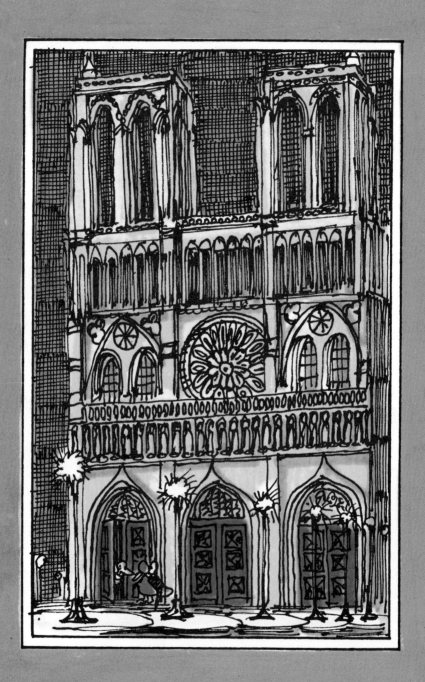

When Miss Mallard and Inspector Widgeon got to Notre Dame, they pounded on a heavy wooden door. Helene Eider opened it for the two ducktectives. They told her why they were there.

"Marie was here earlier," said Helene Eider. "Then she went to see Georgette, who sells flowers at the Eiffel Tower."

"Let's go, Willard," said Miss Mallard.

"Are you sure one of us shouldn't go back and question the can-can girls, Aunty?" asked Inspector Widgeon.

"No, Willard," said Miss Mallard firmly.

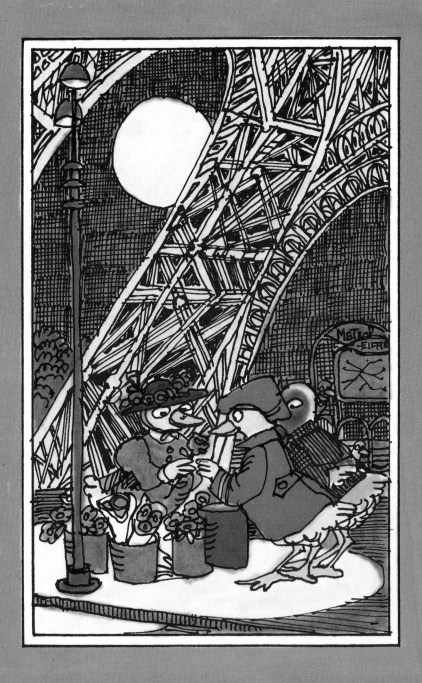

They took the Metro (the Paris subway) to the Eiffel Tower. Georgette was out front selling flowers.

"Marie just left," Georgette told them. "She said that she was going to the Cafe du Nantes in Montmartre to see her friend, Pierre, who works there. Here, have a flower."

"Thank you," said Miss Mallard.

"Maybe *I* should go back and question the can-can girls, Aunty," said Willard.

"Really, Willard!" said Miss Mallard. "Let's go!"

They took another Metro to Montmartre—the artists' section of Paris. They found the Cafe du Nantes on one of the side streets. Pierre, they discovered, was the headwaiter there. He took them to a table at the back of the cafe. There sat Marie!

Miss Mallard told Marie why they had come looking for her.

"I checked the suitcase at the Gare de Lyon," said Marie. "That's because I know the attendant there and trust him."

Miss Mallard and Inspector Widgeon thanked her and quickly left the cafe.

Outside, Miss Mallard said, "What if we were able to catch the thieves and retrieve Claudine's suitcase at the same time, Willard?"

"How?" asked Inspector Widgeon.

"Here's what we'll do," said Miss Mallard. "Take this key to my hotel room. Find my empty suitcase and put this knitting bag of mine inside. Check the suitcase at the Gare de Lyon. Take the claim ticket to Claudine and ask her to bring it with her to the station. I will meet her there and explain everything. You wait for us at the Canard-Rouge."

One hour later, Miss Mallard stood in a dark corner of the waiting room at the Gare de Lyon. At last, she saw Claudine come in and called to her.

"Were you followed?" asked Miss Mallard.

"Yes, I was," said Claudine. "What is this about?"

"I need your help," said Miss Mallard. "Go and claim my suitcase with the ticket that Willard gave you."

"But what about *my* suitcase?" asked Claudine.

"I still have the ticket for it," said Miss Mallard. "But first we've got to catch the thieves."

Claudine did as Miss Mallard asked. She went to the baggage claim and collected Miss Mallard's suitcase. Then she started walking back to the waiting room. She was halfway across the room when suddenly someone rushed at her from behind and grabbed the suitcase. The robber ran with it to the street exit.

"Help! *Gendarme!*" cried Claudine.

A policeman came running.

Miss Mallard was waiting by the exit. She saw the robber about to jump into a waiting taxi.

"There he is, officer!" she called.

The policeman stopped the robber before he had a chance to get away with the suitcase.

Claudine came out onto the street.

"I know him!" she cried. "He is Philippe Souchet! He is a waiter at the Canard-Rouge!"

"Right!" said Miss Mallard. "And his partner is inside the taxi."

Claudine looked inside the taxi.

"Gerard Tadorne—our stage doorman!" exclaimed Claudine.

"Yes," said Miss Mallard. "I thought it strange that a stage doorman wasn't on duty when Willard and I first went backstage. They always stay at their post in any emergency. He was the ducknapper."

"I don't know what you are talking about," said Gerard Tadorne. "This suitcase is ours, officer."

"If that's true," said the policeman, "what's inside it?"

"A costume," said Philippe.

"That's right," said Gerard. "A friend of ours asked us to claim it for her."

The policeman turned to Miss Mallard and Claudine and asked, "And what do you say?"

"It has my knitting bag inside," said Miss Mallard.

"Mmmm," said the policeman. "Let's take it to the station master's office and see who's telling the truth."

In the office, the policeman snapped open the suitcase.

"What's this?" asked the policeman.

"My knitting bag," said Miss Mallard.

Gerard and Philippe started to run.

"Hold it!" said the policeman.

"We made a mistake," said Gerard. "We thought it was our suitcase."

"You are both under arrest," said the policeman, "for attempting to commit robbery. I'm taking you to police headquarters."

"Be sure to take their wing prints," said Miss Mallard. "I believe you'll find that Philippe's prints match the prints of the international jewel thief called 'the Red Carnation.'"

The policeman took the crooks away.

"Phooey!" said Gerard to Philippe as they were leaving. "I told you that this wild scheme of yours would never work."

"Humph!" said Philippe. "This is what I get for asking *you* to help. I should have done it myself."

Miss Mallard and Claudine watched them leave.

"How can I ever thank you, Miss Mallard," said Claudine. "But are my suitcase and grandmother's jeweled costume safe?"

"Let's go and see," said Miss Mallard.

They went to the baggage claim and presented the ticket.

"That's it!" said Claudine. "That's my suitcase. And here's the key to open it. I've kept it on a chain around my neck."

They set the suitcase on a bench and opened it. Inside was the costume covered with jewels.

"*Ooo-la-la!*" said Claudine. "See how the jewels sparkle! Grandmother will be so happy to hear that they are safe. I'm so grateful to you, Miss Mallard."

"It wouldn't have been possible without you," said Miss Mallard.

With that they left the station to go back to the Canard-Rouge in time for Claudine's next show.

Back at the Canard-Rouge, Miss
Mallard went to find Inspector Widgeon to
tell him that the case was solved. He was
backstage chatting with the can-can girls,
so Miss Mallard went out front to watch
the show alone.

And then, who should she find at her
table but the policeman who made the
arrest!

"I'm off duty now," he said. "I thought
we could celebrate together."

"I would be pleased as punch," said Miss
Mallard. "In fact, I think I'll have some—
instead of my usual tea."